D0592956

STORIES OF
PEACE AND WAR

TRYING MOMENTS

STORIES OF
PEACE AND WAR

By
Frederic Remington, 1861-1909.

02118006193369

Short Story Index Reprint Series

BOOKS FOR LIBRARIES PRESS
FREEPORT, NEW YORK

First Published 1899
Reprinted 1970

STANDARD BOOK NUMBER:
8369-3604-3

LIBRARY OF CONGRESS CATALOG CARD NUMBER:
75-125237

PRINTED IN THE UNITED STATES OF AMERICA

THE STRANGE DAYS THAT CAME TO JIMMIE FRIDAY

The Strange Days that Came to Jimmie Friday

THE "Abwee-chemun" * Club was organized with six charter members at a heavy lunch in the Savarin restaurant — one of those lunches which make through connections to dinner without change. One member basely deserted, while two more lost all their enthusiasm on the following morning, but three of us stuck. We vaguely knew that somewhere north of the Canadian Pacific and south of Hudson Bay were big lakes and rapid rivers—lakes whose names we did not know; lakes bigger than Champlain, with unnamed rivers between them. We did not propose

* Algonquin for "paddle and canoe."

3

to be boated around in a big birch-bark by two voyagers among blankets and crackers and ham, but each provided himself a little thirteen-foot cedar canoe, twenty-nine inches in the beam, and weighing less than forty pounds. I cannot tell you precisely how our party was sorted, but one was a lawyer with eye-glasses and settled habits, loving nature, though detesting canoes; the other was nominally a merchant, but in reality an atavic Norseman of the wolf and raven kind; while I am not new. Together we started.

Presently the Abwees sat about the board of a lumbermen's hotel, filled with house-flies and slatternly waiter-girls, who talked familiarly while they served greasy food. The Abwees were yet sore in their minds at the thoughts of the smelly beds upstairs, and discouragement sat deeply on their souls. But their time was not yet.

After breakfast they marched to the Hudson Bay Company's store, knowing as they did that in Canada there are only two places for a traveller to go who wants anything—the great company or the parish priest; and then, having explained to the factor their dream, they were told "that beyond, beyond some days' journey"—oh! that awful beyond, which for centuries has stood across the path of the pioneer, and in these latter days confronts the sportsman and wilderness lover—"that beyond some days' journey to the north was a country such as they had dreamed—up Temiscamingue and beyond."

The subject of a guide was considered.

Jimmie Friday always brought a big toboggan-load of furs into Fort Tiemogamie every spring, and was accounted good in his business. He and his big brother trapped together, and in turn followed the ten days' swing through the snow-laden forest which they had covered with their dead-falls and steel-jawed traps; but when the ice went out in the rivers, and the great pines dripped with the melting snows, they had nothing more to do but cut a few cords of wood for their widowed mother's cabin near the post. Then the brother and he paddled down to Bais des Pierres, where the brother engaged as a deck hand on a steamboat, and Jimmie hired himself as a guide for some bushrangers, as the men are called who explore for pine lands for the great lumber firms. Having worked all summer and got through with that business, Jimmie bethought him to dissipate for a few days in the bustling lumber town down on the Ottawa River. He had been there before to feel the exhilaration of civilization, but beyond that clearing he had never known anything more inspiring than

a Hudson Bay post, which is gener-
ally a log store, a house where the
agent lives, and a few tiny Indian
cabins set higgledy-piggledy in a
sunburnt gash of stumps and bowlders, lost in the middle of the
solemn, unresponsive forest. On
this morning in question he had
stepped from his friend's cabin up
in the Indian village, and after light-
ing a perfectly round and rather
yellow cigar, he had instinctively
wandered down to the Hudson Bay
store, there to find himself amused
by a strange sight.

The Abwees had hired two French-
Indian voyagers of sinister mien, and
a Scotch-Canadian boy bred to the
bush. They were out on the grass,
engaged in taking burlaps off three
highly polished canoes, while the
clerk from the store ran out and
asked questions about " how much
bacon," and " will fifty pounds of
pork be enough, sir ? "

The round yellow cigar was getting stubby, while Jimmie's modest eyes sought out the points of interest in the new-comers, when he was suddenly and sharply addressed :

" Can you cook ? "

Jimmie could n't do anything in a hurry, except chop a log in two, paddle very fast, and shoot quickly, so he said, as was his wont,

" I think—I dun'no'— "

" Well—how much ? " came the query.

" Two daul—ars— " said Jimmie.

The transaction was complete. The yellow butt went over the fence, and Jimmie shed his coat. He was directed to lend a hand by the bustling sportsmen, and requested to run and find things of which he had never before in his life heard the name.

After two days' travel the Abwees were put ashore—boxes, bags, rolls of blankets, canoes, Indians, and plunder of many sorts—on a pebbly beach, and the steamer backed off and steamed away. They had reached the " beyond " at last, and the odoriferous little bedrooms, the bustle of the preparation, the cares of their lives, were behind. Then there was a girding up of the loins, a getting out of tump-lines and canvas packs, and the long portage was begun.

The voyagers carried each two hundred pounds as they stalked away into the wilderness, while the attorney-at-law " hefted " his pack, wiped his eye-glasses with his pocket-handkerchief, and tried cheerfully to assume the responsibilities of " a dead game sport."

" I cannot lift the thing, and how I am going to carry it is more than I know; but I 'm a dead game sport, and I am going to try. I do not want to be dead game, but it looks as though I could n't help it. Will some gentleman help me to adjust this cargo ? "

The night overtook the outfit in an old beaver meadow half-way through the trail. Like all first camps, it was tough. The lean-to tents went up awkwardly. No one could find anything. Late at night the Abwees lay on their backs under the blankets, while the fog settled over the meadow and blotted out the stars.

On the following day the stuff was all gotten through, and by this time the lawyer had become a voyager, willing to carry anything he could stagger under. It is strange how one can accustom himself to "pack." He may never use the tump-line, since it goes across the head, and will unseat his intellect if he does, but with shoulder-straps and a tumpline a man who thinks he is not strong will simply amaze himself inside of a week by what he can do. As for our little canoes, we could trot with them. Each Abwee carried his own belongings and his boat, which entitled him to the distinction of " a dead game sport," whatever that may mean, while the Indians portaged their larger canoes and our mass of supplies, making many trips backward and forward in the process.

At the river everything was parcelled out and arranged. The birch-barks were repitched, and every man found out what he was expected to portage and do about camp. After breaking and making camp three times, the outfit could pack up, load the canoes, and move inside of fifteen minutes. At the first camp the lawyer essayed his canoe, and was cautioned that the delicate thing might flirt with him. He stepped in and sat gracefully down in about two feet of water, while the " delicate thing " shook herself saucily at his side. After he had crawled dripping ashore and wiped his eye-glasses, he engaged to sell the "delicate thing" to an Indian for one dollar and a half on a promissory note. The trade was suppressed, and he was urged to try again. A man who has held down a cane-bottom chair conscientiously for fifteen years looks askance at so fickle a thing as a canoe twenty-nine inches in the beam. They are nearly as hard to sit on in the water as a cork ; but once one is in the bottom they are stable enough, though they do not submit to liberties or palsied movements. The staid lawyer was filled with horror at the prospect of another go at his polished beauty; but, remembering his resolve to be dead game, he abandoned his life to the chances, and got in this time safely.

So the Abwees went down the river on a golden morning, their double-blade paddles flashing in the sun and sending the drip in a shower on the glassy water. The smoke from the lawyer's pipe hung behind him in the quiet air, while the note of the reveille clangored from the little buglette of the Norseman. Jimmie and the big Scotch backwoodsman swayed their bodies in one boat, while the two sinister voyagers dipped their paddles in the big canoe.

The Norseman's gorge came up, and he yelled back: " Say! this suits me. I am never going back to New York."

Jimmie grinned at the noise; it made him happy. Such a morning, such a water, such a lack of anything ʋ disturb one's peace! Let man's better nature revel in the beauties of existence; they inflate his soul. The colors play upon the senses — the reddish-yellow of the birch-barks, the blue of the water, and the silver sheen as it parts at the bows of the canoes; the dark evergreens, the steely rocks with their lichens, the white trunks of the birches, their fluffy tops so greeny green, and over all the gold of a sunny day. It is my religion, this thing, and I do not know how to tell all I feel concerning it.

The rods were taken out, a gang of flies put on and trolled behind— but we have all seen a man fight a five-pound bass for twenty minutes. The waters fairly swarmed with them, and we could always get enough for the " pot " in a half-hour's fishing at any time during the trip. The Abwecs were canoeing, not hunting or fishing; though, in truth, they did not need to hunt spruce-partridge or fish for bass in any sporting sense; they simply went out after them, and never stayed over half an hour. On a point we stopped for lunch: the Scotchman always struck the beach a-cooking. He had a " kit " which was a big camp-pail, and inside of it were more dishes than are to be found in some hotels. He broiled the bacon, instead of frying it, and thus we were saved the terrors of indigestion. He had many luxuries in his commissary, among them dried apples, with which he filled a camp-pail one day and put them on to boil. They subsequently got to be about a foot deep all over the camp, while Furguson stood around and regarded the black-magic of the thing with overpowering emotions and Homeric tongue. Furguson was a good genius, big and gentle, and a woodsman root and branch. The ^bwees had intended their days in the wilderness to be happy singing flights of time, but with grease and paste in one's stomach what may not befall the mind when it is bent on nature's doings ?

And thus it was that the gloomy Indian Jimmie Friday, despite his tuberculosis begotten of insufficient nourishment, was happy in these strange days—even to the extent of looking with wondrous eyes on the nooks which we loved—nooks which previously for him had only sheltered possible " dead-falls " or not, as the discerning eye of the trapper decided the prospects for pelf.

Going ashore on a sandy beach, Jimmie wandered down its length, his hunter mind seeking out the footprints of his prey. He stooped down, and then beckoned me to come, which I did.

Pointing at the sand, he said, " You know him ? "

" Wolves," I answered.

" Yes—first time I see 'em up here—they be follerin' the deers—bad—bad. No can trap 'em—verrie smart."

A half-dozen wolves had chased a deer into the water; but wolves do not take to the water, so they had stopped and drank, and then gone rollicking together up the beach. There were cubs, and one great track as big as a mastiff might make.

" See that—moose track—he go by yesterday "; and Jimmie pointed to enormous footprints in the muck of a marshy place. " Verrie big moose—we make call at next camp —think it is early for call."

At the next camp Jimmie made the usual birch-bark moose-call, and at evening blew it, as he also did on the following morning. This camp was a divine spot on a rise back of a long sandy beach, and we concluded to stop for a day. The Norseman and I each took a man in our canoes and started out to explore. I wanted to observe some musk-rat hotels down in a big marsh, and the Norseman was fishing. The attorney was content to sit on a log by the shores of the lake, smoke lazily, and watch the sun shimmer through the lifting fog. He saw a canoe approaching

B

from across the lake. He gazed vacantly at it, when it grew strange and more unlike a canoe. The paddles did not move, but the phantom craft drew quickly on.

" Say, Furguson — come here — look at that canoe."

The Scotchman came down, with a pail in one hand, and looked. " Canoe—hell—it 's a moose—and there ain't a pocket-pistol in this camp," and he fairly jumped up and down.

" You don't say—you really don't say ! " gasped the lawyer, who now began to exhibit signs of insanity.

" Yes—he 's going to be d——d sociable with us—he 's coming right bang into this camp."

The Indian too came down, but he was long past talking English, and the gutturals came up in lumps, as though he was trying to keep them down.

The moose finally struck a long

point of sand and rushes about two hundred yards away, and drew majestically out of the water, his hide dripping, and the sun glistening on his antlers and back.

The three men gazed in spellbound admiration at the picture until the moose was gone. When they had recovered their senses they slowly went up to the camp on the ridge— disgusted and dumfounded.

" I could almost put a cartridge in that old gun-case and kill him," sighed the backwoodsman.

" I have never hunted in my life," mused the attorney, " but few men have seen such a sight," and he filled his pipe.

" Hark—listen! " said the Indian. There was a faint cracking, which presently became louder. " He 's coming into camp "; and the Indian nearly died from excitement as he grabbed a hatchet. The three unfortunate men stepped to the back of the tents, and as big a bull moose as walks the lonely woods came up to within one hundred and fifty feet of the camp, and stopped, returning their gaze.

Thus they stood for what they say was a minute, but which seemed like hours. The attorney composedly admired the unusual sight. The Indian and Furguson swore softly but most viciously until the moose moved away. The Indian hurled the hatchet at the retreating figure, with a final curse, and the thing was over.

"Those fellows who are out in their canoes will be sick abed when we tell them what 's been going on in the camp this morning," sighed Mr. Furguson, as he scoured a cooking-pot.

I fear we would have had that moose on our consciences if we had been there: the game law was not up at the time, but I should have asked for strength from a higher source than my respect for law.

The golden days passed and the lake grew great. The wind blew at our backs. The waves rolled in restless surges, piling the little canoes on their crests and swallowing them in the troughs. The canoes thrashed the water as they flew along, half in, half out, but they rode like ducks. The Abwees took off their hats, gripped their double blades, made the water swirl behind them, howled in glee to each other through the rushing storm. To be five miles from shore in a seaway in kayaks like ours was a sensation. We found they stood it well, and grew contented. It was the complement to the golden lazy days when the water was glass, and the canoes rode upside down over its mirror surface. The Norseman grinned and shook his head in token of his pleasure, much as an epicure might after a sip of superior Burgundy.

" How do you fancy this ? " we asked the attorney-at-law.

" I am not going to deliver an opinion until I get ashore. I would never have believed that I would be here at my time of life, but one never knows what a —— fool one can make of one's self. My glasses are covered with water, and I can hardly see, but I can't let go of this paddle to wipe them," shrieked the man of the office chair, in the howl of the weather.

But we made a long journey by the aid of the wind, and grew a contempt for it. How could one imagine the stability of those little boats until one had tried it ?

That night we put into a natural harbor and camped on a gravel beach. The tents were up and the supper cooking, when the wind hauled and blew furiously into our haven. The fires were scattered and the rain came in blinding sheets. The tent-pegs pulled from the sand. We sprang to our feet and held on to the poles, wet to the skin. It was useless; the rain blew right under the canvas. We laid the tents on the " grub " and stepped out into the dark. We could not be any wetter, and we did not care. To stand in the dark in the wilderness, with nothing to eat, and a fire-engine playing a hose on you for a couple of hours—if you have imagination enough, you can fill in the situation. But the gods were propitious. The wind died down. The stars came out by myriads. The fires were re-lighted, and the ordinary life begun. It was late in the night before our clothes, blankets, and tents were dry but, like boys, we forgot it all.

Then came a river—blue and flat like the sky above—running through rushy banks, backed by the masses of the forest; anon the waters rushed upon us over the rocks, and we fought, plunk-plunk-plunk, with the paddles, until our strength gave out. We stepped out into the water, and getting our lines, and using our long double blades as fenders, " tracked " the canoes up through the boil. The Indians in their heavier boats used " setting-poles " with marvellous dexterity, and by furious exertion were able to draw steadily up the grade — though at times they too " tracked," and even portaged. Our largest canoe weighed two hundred pounds, but a little voyager managed to lug it, though how I could n't comprehend, since his pipe-stem legs fairly bent and wobbled under the enormous ark. None of us by this time were able to lift the loads which we carried, but, like a Western pack-mule, we stood about and had things piled on to us, until nothing more would stick. Some of the back-woodsmen carry incredible masses of stuff, and their lore is full of tales which no one could be expected to believe. Our men did not hesitate to take two hundred and fifty pounds over short portages, which were very rough and stony, though they all said if they slipped they expected to break a leg. This is largely due to the tump-line, which is laid over the head, while persons unused to it must have shoulder-straps in addition, which are not as good, because the " breastbone," so called, is not strong enough.

We were getting day by day farther into " the beyond." There were no traces here of the hand of man. Only Jimmie knew the way —it was his trapping-ground. Only once did we encounter people. We were blown into a little board dock, on a gray day, with the waves piling up behind us, and made a difficult landing. Here were a few tiny log houses—an outpost of the Hudson Bay Company. We renewed our stock of provisions, after laborious trading with the stagnated people who live in the lonely place. There was nothing to sell us but a few of the most common necessities; however, we needed only potatoes and sugar. This was Jimmie's home. Here we saw his poor old mother, who was being tossed about in the smallest of canoes as she drew her nets. Jimmie's father had gone on a hunting expedition and had never come back. Some day Jimmie's old mother will go out on the wild lake to tend her nets, and she will not come back. Some time Jimmie too will not return — for this Indian struggle with nature is appalling in its fierceness.

There was a dance at the post, which the boys attended, going by canoe at night, and they came back early in the morning, with much giggling at their gallantries.

The loneliness of this forest life is positively discouraging to think about. What the long winters must be in the little cabins I cannot imagine, and I fear the traders must be all avarice, or have none at all; for there can certainly be absolutely no intellectual life. There is undoubtedly work, but not one single problem concerning it. The Indian hunters do fairly well in a financial way, though their lives are beset with weakening hardships and constant danger. Their meagre diet wears out their constitutions, and they are subject to disease. The simplicity of their minds makes it very difficult to see into their life as they try to narrate it to one who may be interested.

From here on was through beautiful little lakes, and the voyagers rigged blanket sails on the big canoes, while we towed behind. Then came the river and the rapids, which we ran, darting between rocks, bumping on sunken stones—shooting fairly out into the air, all but turning over hundreds of times. One day the Abwees glided out in the big lake Tesmiaquemang, and saw the steamer going to Bais des Pierres. We hailed her, and she stopped, while the little canoes danced about in the swell as we were loaded one by one. On the deck above us the passengers admired a kind of boat the like of which had not before appeared in these parts.

At Bais des Pierres we handed over the residue of the commissaries of the Abwee-Chemun to Jimmie Friday, including personally many pairs of well - worn golf - breeches, sweaters, rubber coats, knives which would be proscribed by law in New York. If Jimmie ever parades his solemn wilderness in these garbs, the owls will laugh from the trees. Our simple forest friend laid in his winter stock—traps, flour, salt, tobacco, and pork, a new axe—and accompanied us back down the lake again on the steamer. She stopped in mid-stream, while Jimmie got his bundles into his " bark " and shoved off, amid a hail of " good-byes."

The engine palpitated, the big wheel churned the water astern, and we drew away. Jimmie bent on his paddle with the quick body-swing habitual to the Indian, and after a time grew a speck on the reflection of the red sunset in Temiscamingue.

The Abwees sat sadly leaning on the after-rail, and agreed that Jimmie was " a lovely Injun." Jimmie had gone into the shade of the overhang of the cliffs, when the Norseman started violently up, put his hands in his pockets, stamped his foot, and said, " By George, fellows, any D. F. would call this a sporting trip!"

JOSHUA GOODENOUGH'S
OLD LETTER

THE MARCH OF ROGER'S RANGERS

Joshua Goodenough's Old Letter

THE following letter has come into my possession, which I publish because it is history, and descends to the list of those humble beings who builded so well for us the institutions which we now enjoy in this country. It is yellow with age, and much frayed out at the foldings, being in those spots no longer discernible. It runs:

ALBANY *June* 1798.

TO MY DEAR SON JOSEPH.—It is true that there are points in the history of the country in which your father had a concern in his early life and as you ask me to put it down I will do so briefly. Not however,

c

my dear Joseph, as I was used to tell it to you when you were a lad, but with more exact truth, for I am getting on in my years and this will soon be all that my posterity will have of their ancestor. I conceive that now the descendents of the noble band of heroes who fought off the indians, the Frenche and the British will prevail in this country, and my children's children may want to add what is found here in written to their own achievements.

To begin with, my father was the master of a fishing - schooner, of Marblehead. In the year 1745 he was taken at sea by a French man-of-war off Louisbourg, after making a desperate resistence. His ship was in a sinking condition and the blood was mid-leg deep on her deck. Your grandfather was an upstanding man and did not prostrate easily, but the Frencher was too big, so he was captured and later found his way as a prisoner to Quebec. He was exchanged by a mistake in his identity for Huron indians captivated in York, and he subsequently settled near Albany, afterwards bringing my mother, two sisters, and myself from Marblehead.

He engaged in the indian trade, and as I was a rugged lad of my years I did often accompany him on his expeditions westward into the Mohawk townes, thus living in bark camps among Indians and got thereby a knowledge of their ways. I made shift also to learn their language, and what with living in the bush for so many years I was a hand at a pack or paddle and no mean hunter besides. I was put to school for two seasons in Albany which was not to my liking, so I straightway ran off to a hunters camp up the Hudson, and only came back when my father would say that I should not be again put with the pedegogue. For this adventure I had a good strapping from my father, and was set to work in his trade again. My mother was a pious woman and did not like me to grow up in the wilderness—for it was the silly fashion of those times to ape the manners and dress of the Indians.

My father was a shifty trader and very ventursome. He often had trouble with the people in these parts, who were Dutch and were jealous of him. He had a violent temper and was not easily bent from his purpose by opporsition. His men had a deal of fear of him and good cause enough in the bargain, for I once saw him discipline a half-negro man who was one of his boatmen for stealing his private jug of liquor from his private pack. He clinched with the negro and soon had him on the ground, where the man struggled manfully but to no purpose for your grandfather soon had him at his mercy. " Now " said he " give me the jug or take the consequences.'' The other boat paddlers wanted to rescue him but I menaced them with my fusil and the matter ended by the return of the jug.

In 1753 he met his end at the hands of western indians in the French interest, who shot him as he was helping to carry a battoe, and he was burried in the wilderness. My mother then returned to her home in Massassachusetts, journeying with a party of traders but I staid with the Dutch on these frontiers because I had learned the indian trade and liked the country. Not having any chances, I had little book learning in my youth, having to this day a regret concerning it. I read a few books, but fear I had a narrow knowledge of things outside the Dutch settlements. On the frontiers, for that matter, few people had much skill with the pen, nor was much needed. The axe and rifle, the paddle and pack being more to our hands in those rough days. To prosper though, men weare shrewd-headed enough. I have never seen that books helped people to trade sharper. Shortly afterwards our trade fell away, for the French had embroiled the Indians against us. Crown Point was the Place from which the Indians in their interest had been fitted out to go against our settlements, so a design was formed by His Majesty the British King to dispossess them of that place. Troops were levid in the Province and the war began. The Frenchers had the best of the fighting.

Our frontiers were beset with the Canada indians so that it was not safe to go about in the country at all. I was working for Peter Vrooman, a trader, and was living at his house on the Mohawk. One Sunday morning I found a negro boy who was shot through the body with two balls as he was hunting for stray sheep, and all this within half a mile of Vrooman's house. Then an express came up the valley who left word that the Province was levying troops at Albany to fight the French, and I took my pay from Vrooman saying that I would go to Albany for a soldier. Another young man and myself paddled down to Albany, and we both enlisted in the York levies. We drawed our ammunition tents, kettles, bowls and knives at the Albany flats, and were drilled by an officer who had been in her Majesty's Service. One man was given five hundred lashes for enlisting in some Connecticut troops, and the orders said that any man who should leave His Majesty's service without a Regular discharge should suffer Death. The restraint which was put upon me by this military life was not to my liking, and I was in a mortal dread of the whippings which men were constantly receiving for breaches of the discipline. I felt that I could not survive the shame of being trussed up and lashed before men's eyes, but I did also have a great mind to fight the French which kept me along. One day came an order to prepare a list of officers and men who were willing to go scouting and be freed from other duty, and after some time I got my name put down, for I was thought too young, but I said I knew the woods, had often been to Andiatirocte (or Lake George as it had then become the fashion to call it) and they let me go. It was dangerous work, for reports came every day of how our Rangers suffered up country at the hands of the cruel savages from Canada, but it is impossible to play at bowls without

meeting some rubs. A party of us
proceeded up river to join Captain
Rogers at Fort Edward, and we were
put to camp on an Island. This was
in October of the year 1757. We
found the Rangers were rough bor-
derers like ourselvs, mostly Hampshire men well used to the woods and
much accustomed to the Enemy.
They dressed in the fashion of those
times in skin and grey duffle hunting
frocks, and were well armed. Rogers himself was a doughty man and
had a reputation as a bold Ranger
leader. The men declaired that
following him was sore service, but
that he most always met with great
success. The Fort was garrissoned
by His Majesty's soldiers, and I did
not conceive that they were much
fitted for bush-ranging, which I afterwards found to be the case, but they
would always fight well enough,
though often to no good purpose,
which was not their fault so much as

the headstrong leadership which persisted in making them come to close quarters while at a disadvantage. There were great numbers of pack horses coming and going with stores, and many officers in gold lace and red coats were riding about directing here and there. I can remember that I had a great interest in this concourse of men, for up to that time I had not seen much of the world outside of the wilderness. There was terror of the Canada indians who had come down to our borders hunting for scalps—for these were continually lurking near the cantanements to waylay the unwary. I had got acquainted with a Hampshire borderer who had passed his life on the Canada frontier, where he had fought indians and been captured by them. I had seen much of indians and knew their silent forest habits when hunting, so that I felt that when they were after human beings they would be no mean adversaries, but I had never hunted them or they me.

I talked at great length with this Shankland, or Shanks as he was called on account of his name and his long legs, in course of which he explained many useful points to me concerning Ranger ways. He said they always marched until it was quite dark before encamping—that they always returned by a different route from that on which they went out, and that they circled on their trail at intervals so that they might intercept any one coming on their rear. He told me not to gather up close to other Rangers in a fight but to keep spread out, which gave the Enemy less mark to fire upon and also deceived them as to your own numbers. Then also he cautioned me not to fire on the Enemy when we were in ambush till they have approached quite near, which will put them in greater surprise and give your own people time to rush in on them with hatchets or cutlasses. Shanks and I had finally a great fancy for each other and passed most of our time in company. He was a slow man in his movements albeit he could move fast enough on occassion, and was a great hand to take note of things happening around him. No indian was better able to discern a trail in the bush than he, nor could one be found his equal at making snow shoes, carving a powder horn or fashioning any knick-nack he was a mind to set his hand to.

The Rangers were accustomed to scout in small parties to keep the Canada indians from coming close to Fort Edward. I had been out with Shanks on minor occasions, but I must relate my first adventure.

A party . . . (here the writing is lost) . . . was desirous of

taking a captive or scalp. I mis-
doubted our going alone by ourselvs, but he said we were as safe as
with more. We went northwest
slowly for two days, and though we
saw many old trails we found none
which were fresh. We had gone on
until night when we lay bye near a
small brook. I was awakened by
Shanks in the night and heard a
great howling of wolves at some distance off togther with a gun shot.
We lay awake until daybreak and at
intervals heard a gun fired all through
the night. We decided that the firing could not come from a large
party and so began to approach the
sound slowly and with the greatest
caution. We could not understand
why the wolves should be so bold
with the gun firing, but as we came
neare we smelled smoke and knew it
was a camp-fire. There were a number of wolves running about in the
underbrush from whose actions we

located the camp. From a rise we could presently see it, and were surprised to find it contained five Indians all lying asleep in their blankets. The wolves would go right up to the camp and yet the indians did not deign to give them any notice whatsoever, or even to move in the least when one wolf pulled at the blanket of a sleeper. We each selected a man when we had come near enough, and preparing to deliver our fire, when of a sudden one figure rose up slightly. We nevertheless fired and then rushed forward, reloading. To our astonishment none of the figures moved in the least but the wolves scurried off. We were advancing cautiously when Shanks caught me by the arm saying " we must run, that they had all died of the smallpox," and run we did lustilly for a good long distance. After this manner did many Indians die in the wilderness from that dreadful disease, and I have since supposed that the last living indian had kept firing his gun at the wolves until he had no longer strength to reload his piece.

After this Shanks and I had become great friends for he had liked the way I had conducted myself on this expedition. He was always arguying with me to cut off my eelskin que which I wore after the fashion of the Dutch folks, saying that the Canada indians would parade me for a Dutchman after that token was gone with my scalp. He had . . . (writing obliterated).

Early that winter I was one of 150 Rangers who marched with Captain Rogers against the Enemy at Carrillion. The snow was not deep at starting but it continued to snow until it was heavy footing and many of the men gave out and returned to Fort Edward, but notwithstanding my exhaustion I continued on for six days until we were come to within six hundred yards of Carrillion Fort. The captain had made us a speech in which he told us the points where we were to rendevoux if we were broke in the fight, for further resistence until night came on, when we could take ourselvs off as best we might. I was with the advance guard. We lay in ambush in some fallen timber quite close to a road, from which we could see the smoke from the chimneys of the Fort and the centries walking their beats. A French soldier was seen to come from the Fort and the word was passed to let him go bye us, as he came down the road. We lay perfectly still not daring to breathe, and though he saw nothing he stopped once and seemed undecided as to going on, but suspecting nothing he continued and was captured by our people below, for prisoners were wanted at Headquarters to give information of the French forces and intentions.

A man taken in this way was threatened with Death if he did not tell the whole truth, which under the circumstancs he mostly did to save his life.

The French did not come out of the Fort after us, though Rogers tried to entice them by firing guns and showing small parties of men which feigned to retreat. We were ordered to destroy what we could of the supplies, so Shanks and I killed a small cow which we found in the edge of the clearing and took off some fresh beef of which food we were sadly in need, for on these scouts the Rangers were not permitted to fire guns at game though it was found in thir path, as it often was in fact. I can remember on one occassion that I stood by a tree in a snow storm, with my gun depressed under my frock the better to keep it dry, when I was minded to glance quickly around and there saw a large

D

49

wolf just ready to spring upon me.
I cautiously presented my fusee but
did not dare to fire against the orders.
An other Ranger came shortly into
view and the wolf took himself off.
We burned some large wood piles,
which no doubt made winter work
for to keep some Frenchers at home.
They only fired some cannon at us,
which beyond a great deal of noise
did no harm. We then marched
back to Fort Edward and were glad
enough to get there, since it was
time for snow-shoes, which we had
not with us.

The Canada indians were coming
down to our Forts and even behind
them to intercept our convoys or any
parties out on the road, so that the
Rangers were kept out, to head them
when they could, or get knowledge
of their whereabouts. Shanks and I
went out with two Mohegon indians
on a scout. It was exceedingly
stormy weather and very heavy

travelling except on the River. I had got a bearskin blanket from the indians which is necessary to keep out the cold at this season. We had ten days of bread, pork and rum with a little salt with us, and followed the indians in a direction North-and-bye-East toward the lower end of Lake Champlain, always keeping to the high-ground with the falling snow to fill our tracks behind us. For four days we travelled when we were well up the west side. We had crossed numbers of trails but they were all full of old snow and not worth regarding—still we were so far from our post that in event of encountering any numbers of the Enemy we had but small hope of a safe return and had therefore to observe the greatest caution.

As we were making our way an immense painter so menaced us that we were forced to fire our guns to dispatch him. He was found to be very old, his teeth almost gone, and was in the last stages of starvation. We were much alarmed at this mis-adventure, fearing the Enemy might hear us or see the ravens gathering above, so we crossed the Lake that night on some new ice to blind our trail, where I broke through in one place and was only saved by Shanks, who got hold of my eel-skin que, thereby having something to pull me out with. We got into a deep gully, and striking flint made a fire to dry me and I did not suffer much incon-venience.

The day following we took a long circle and came out on the lower end of the Lake, there laying two days in ambush, watching the Lake for any parties coming or going. Before dark a Mohigon came in from watch saying that men were coming down the Lake. We gathered at the point and saw seven of the Enemy come slowly on. There were three indians two Canadians and a French officer. Seeing they would shortly pass under our point of land we made ready to fire, and did deliver one fire as they came nigh, but the guns of our Mohigons failed to explode, they being old and well nigh useless, so that all the damage we did was to kill one indian and wound a Canadian, who was taken in hand by his companions, who made off down the shore and went into the bush. We tried to head them unsuccessfully, and after examining the guns of our indians we feared they were so disabled that we gave up and retreated down the Lake, travelling all night. Near morning we saw a small fire which we spied out only to find a large party of the Enemy, whereat we were much disturbed, for our travelling had exhausted us and we feared the pursuit of a fresh enemy as soon as morning should come to show them our trail. We then made our way as fast as possible until late that night, when we laid down for refreshment. We built no fire but could not sleep for fear of the Enemy for it was a bright moonlight, and sure enough we had been there but a couple of hours when we saw the Enemy coming on our track. We here abandoned our bearskins with what provissions we had left and ran back on our trail toward the advancing party. It was dark in the forest and we hoped they might not discover our back track for some time, thus giving us a longer start. This ruse was successful. After some hours travel I became so exhausted that I stopped to rest, whereat the Mohigans left us, but Shanks bided with me, though urging me to move forward. After a time I got strength to move on. Shanks said the Canadians would come up with us if we did not make fast going of it, and that they would disembowel us or tie us to a tree and burn us as was their usual way, for we could in no wise hope to make head against so large a party. Thus we walked steadily till high noon, when my wretched strength gave out so that I fell down saying I had as leave die there as elsewhere. Shanks followed back on our trail, while I fell into a drouse but was so sore I could not sleep. After a time I heard a shot, and shortly two more, when Shanks came running back to me. He had killed an advancing indian and stopped them for a moment. He kicked me vigorously, telling me to come on, as the indians would soon come on again. I got up, and though I could scarcely move I was minded diligently to persevere after Shanks. Thus we staggered on until near night time, when we again stopped and I fell into a deep sleep, but the enemy did not again come up. On

the following day we got into Fort
Edward, where I was taken with a
distemper, was seized with very
grevious pains in the head and back
and a fever. They let blood and
gave me a physic, but I did not get
well around for some time. For
this sickness I have always been
thankful, otherwise I should have
been with Major Rogers in his unfortunate battle, which has become
notable enough, where he was de-
feated by the Canadians and Indians
and lost nigh all his private men,
only escaping himself by a miracle.
We mourned the loss of many friends
who were our comrades, though it
was not the fault of any one, since
the Enemy had three times the
number of the Rangers and hemmed
them in. Some of the Rangers had
surrendered under promise of Quarter, but we afterwards heard that
they were tied to trees and hacked
to death because the indians had

found a scalp in the breast of a man's hunting frock, thus showing that we could never expect such bloody minded villiains to keep their promises of Quarter.

I was on several scouts against them that winter but encountered nothing worthy to relate excepting the hardships which fell to a Ranger's lot. In June the Army having been gathered we proceeded under Abercromby up the Lake to attack Ticonderoga. I thought at the time that so many men must be invincible, but since the last war I have been taught to know different. There were more Highlanders, Grenadiers, Provincial troops, Artillery and Rangers than the eye could compass, for the Lake was black with their battoes. This concourse proceeded to Ticondaroga where we had a great battle and lost many men, but to no avail since we were forced to return.

The British soldiers were by this

time made servicible for forest war-
fare, since the officers and men had
been forced to rid themselvs of their
useless incumbrances and had cut off
the tails of their long coats till they
scarcely reached below thir middles
—they had also left the women at
the Fort, browned thir gun barrells
and carried thir provisions on their
backs, each man enough for himself,
as was our Ranger custom. The
army was landed at the foot of the
Lake, where the Rangers quickly
drove off such small bodies of
Frenchers and Indians as opposed
us, and we began our march by the
rapids. Rogers men cleared the way
and had a most desperate fight with
some French who were minded to
stop us, but we shortly killed and
captured most of them. We again
fell in with them that afternoon and
were challenged Qui vive but answered that we were French, but
they were not deceived and fired

upon us, after which a hot skirmish insued during which Lord Howe was shot through the breast, for which we were all much depressed, because he was our real leader and had raised great hopes of success for us. The Rangers had liked him because he was wont to spend much time talking with them in thir camps and used also to go on scouts. The Rangers were not over fond of British officers in general.

When the time had come for battle we Rangers moved forward, accompanied by the armed boatmen and the Provincial troops. We drove in the French pickets and came into the open where the trees were felled tops toward us in a mighty abbatis, as thiough blown down by the wind. It was all we could undertake to make our way through the mass, and all the while the great breast-works of the French belched cannon and musket balls while the limbs and

splinters flew around us. Then out
of the woods behind us issued the
heavy red masses of the British
troops advancing in battle array with
purpose to storm with the bayonet.
The maze of fallen trees with their
withered leaves hanging broke their
ranks, and the French Retrenchment
blazed fire and death. They advanced bravely up but all to no good
purpose, and hundreds there met their
death. My dear Joseph I have the will
but not the way to tell you all I saw
that awful afternoon. I have since
been in many battles and skirmishes,
but I never have witnessed such
slaughter and such wild fighting as
the British storm of Ticondaroga.
We became mixed up—Highlanders,
Grenadiers, Light Troops, Rangers
and all, and we beat against that
mass of logs and maze of fallend
timber and we beat in vain. I was
once carried right up to the breast-
work, but we were stopped by the

bristling mass of sharpened branches, while the French fire swept us front and flank. The ground was covered deep with dying men, and as I think it over now I can remember nothing but the fruit bourne by the tree of war, for I looked upon so many wonderous things that July day that I could not set them downe at all. We drew off after seeing that human valor could not take that work. We Rangers then skirmished with the French colony troops and the Canada indians until dark while our people rescued the wounded, and then we fell back. The Army was utterly demoralized and made a headlong retreat, during which many wounded men were left to die in the woods. Shanks and I paddled a light bark canoe down the Lake next day, in the bottom of which lay a wounded British officer attended by his servant.

I took my discharge, and lived

until the following Spring with
Vrooman at German Flats, when I
had a desire to go again to the more
active service of the Rangers, for
living in camps and scouting, notwithstanding its dangers, was agree-
able to my taste in those days. So
back to Albany I started, and there
met Major Rogers, whom I acquainted with my desire to again
join his service, whereat he seemed
right glad to put me downe. I ac-
cordingly journeyed to Crown Point,
where I went into camp. I had
bought me a new fire-lock at Albany
which was provided with a bayonet.
It was short, as is best fitted for the
bush, and about 45 balls to the
pound. I had shot it ten times on
trial and it had not failed to discharge at each pull. There was a
great change in the private men of
the Rangers, so many old ones had
been frost bitten and gone home. I
found my friend Shanks, who had

staid though he had been badly frosted during the winter. He had such a hate of the Frenchers and particularly of the Canada Indians that he would never cease to fight them, they having killed all his relatives in New Hampshire which made him bitter against them, he always saying that they might as well kill him and thus make an end of the family.

In June I went north down Champlain with 250 Rangers and Light Infantry in sloop - vessels. The Rangers were . . . (writing lost) . . . but it made no difference. The party was landed on the west side of the Lake near Isle au Noix and lay five days in the bush, it raining hard all the time. I was out with a recoinnoitering party to watch the Isle, and very early in the morning we saw the French coming to our side in boats, whereat we acquainted Major Rogers that the

French were about to attack us. We were drawn up in line to await their coming. The forest always concealed a Ranger line, so that there might not have been a man within a hundred miles for all that could be seen, and so it was that an advance party of the Enemy walked into our line and were captured, which first appraised the French of our position. They shortly attacked us on our left, but I was sent with a party to make our way through a swamp in order to attack their rear. This we accomplished so quietly that we surprized some Canada indians who were lying back of the French line listening to a prophet who was incanting. These we slew, and after our firing many French grenadiers came running past, when they broke before our line. I took a French-man prisoner, but he kept his bayonet pointed at me, all the time yelling in French which I did not understand, though I had my loaded gun pointed at him. He seemed to be disturbed at the sight of a scalp which I had hanging in my belt. I had lately took it from the head of an Indian, it being my first, but I was not minded to kill the poor Frenchman and was saying so in English. He put down his fire-lock finally and offered me his flask to drink liquor with him, but I did not use it. I had known that Shanks carried poisoned liquor in his pack, with the hope that it would destroy any indians who might come into possession of it, if he was taken, whether alive or dead. As I was escorting the Frenchman back to our boats he quickly ran away from me, though I snapped my fire-lock at him, which failed to explode, it having become wet from the rain. Afterwards I heard that a Ranger had shot him, seeing him running in the bush.

We went back to our boats after this victory and took all our wounded and dead with us, which last we buried on an island. Being joined by a party of Stockbridge Indians we were again landed, and after marching for some days came to a road where we recoinnoitered St. John's Fort but did not attack it, Rogers judging it not to be takeable with our force. From here we began to march so fast that only the strongest men could keep up, and at day-break came to another Fort. We ran into the gate while a hay-waggon was passing through, and surprised and captured all the garrison, men women and children. After we had burned and destroyed everything we turned the women and children adrift, but drove the men along as prisoners, making them carry our packs. We marched so fast that the French grenadiers could not keep up, for their breeches were too tight for them to march with ease, whereat we cut off the legs of them with our knives, when they did better. After this expedition we scouted from Crown Point in canoes, Shanks and myself going as far north as we dared toward Isle au Noix, and one day while lying on the bank we saw the army coming. It was an awsome sight to see so many boats filled with brave uniforms, as they danced over the waves. The Rangers and indians came a half a mile ahead of the Army in whale-boats all in line abreast, while behind them came the light Infantry and Grenadiers with Provincial troops on the flanks and Artillery and Store boats bringing up the Rear.

Shanks and I fell in with the Ranger boats, being yet in our small bark and much hurled about by the waves, which rolled prodigious.

The Army continued up the Lake

and drove the Frenchers out of their Forts, they not stopping to resist us till we got to Chamblee, where we staid. But the French in Canada had all surrendered to the British and the war was over. This ended my service as a Ranger in those parts. I went back to Vroomans intending to go again into the indian trade, for now we hoped that the French would no longer be able to stop our enterprises.

Now, my dear son—I will send you this long letter, and will go on writing of my later life in the Western country and in the War of Independence, and will send you those letters as soon as I have them written. I did not do much or occupy a commanding position, but I served faithfully in what I had to do. For the present God bless you my dear son.

JOSHUA GOODENOUGH.

CHASING A MAJOR-GENERAL

Chasing a Major=General

THE car had been side-tracked at Fort Keough, and on the following morning the porter shook me, and announced that it was five o'clock. An hour later I stepped out on the rear platform, and observed that the sun would rise shortly, but that meanwhile the air was chill, and that the bald, square-topped hills of the " bad lands " cut rather hard against the gray of the morning. Presently a trooper galloped up with three led horses, which he tied to a stake. I inspected them, and saw that one had a " cow saddle," which I recognized as an experiment suggested by the general. The animal bearing it had a threatening look, and I expected a repetition of a performance of a few days before, when I had chased the general for over three hours, making in all twenty-eight miles.

Before accepting an invitation to accompany an Indian commission into the Northwest I had asked the general quietly if this was a " horse-back " or a " wagon outfit." He had assured me that he was not a " wagon man," and I indeed had heard before that he was not. There is always a distinction in the army between wagon men and men who go without wagons by transporting their supplies on pack animals. The wagon men have always acquired more reputation as travellers than Indian fighters. In a trip to the Pine Ridge Agency I had discovered that General Miles was not committed to any strained theory of how mounted men should be moved. Any settled purpose he might have about his movements were all locked up in a desperate desire to "get thar." Being a little late in leaving a point on the railroad, I rode along with Lieutenant Guilfoil, of the Ninth, and we moved at a gentle trot. Presently we met a citizen in a wagon, and he, upon observing the lieutenant in uniform, pulled up his team and excitedly inquired,

"What 's the matter, Mr. Soldier?"

Guilfoil said nothing was the matter that he knew of.

"Who be you uns after?"

"No one," replied the lieutenant.

"Well, I just saw a man go whirling up this 'ere valley with a soldier tearin' after him fit to kill" (that was the general's orderly), "and then comes a lot more soldiers just a-smokin', and I sort of wondered what the man had done."

We laughed, and remarked that

73

the general must be riding pretty hard. Other citizens we met inquired if that man was a lunatic or a criminal. The idea of the soldiers pursuing a man in citizen's clothes furthered the idea, but we assured them that it was only General Miles going somewhere.

All of these episodes opened my eyes to the fact that if I followed General Miles I would have to do some riding such as I had rarely done before. In coming back to the railroad we left the Pine Ridge Agency in the evening without supper, and I was careful to get an even start. My horse teetered and wanted to gallop, but I knew that the twenty-eight miles would have to be done at full speed, so I tried to get him down to a fast trot, which gait I knew would last better· but in the process of calming him down to a trot I lost sight of the general and his orderly as they went tearing like mad over a hill against the last gleam of the sunset. I rode at a very rapid trot over the hills in the moonlight for over three hours, but I never saw the general again until I met him at dinner. Then I further concluded that if I followed the general I would have no time to regait my horses, but must take them as I found them, gallop or trot. So on this cool morning at Keough I took observations of the horses which were tied to the post, with my mind full of misgivings.

Patter, patter, patter — clank, clank, clank; up comes the company of Cheyenne scouts who are to escort the general—fine-looking, tall young men, with long hair, and mounted on small Indian ponies. They were dressed and accoutred as United States soldiers, and they fill the eye of a military man until nothing is lacking. Now the general steps out of the car and hands the

commission into a six-mule ambulance. I am given a horse, and,
mounting, we move off over the
plain and into the hills. The sun
comes streaming over the landscape,
and the general is thinking about
this old trail, and how years before
he had ploughed his way through
the blinding snow to the Lame Deer
fight. I am secretly wishing that it
would occupy his mind more fully,
so that my breakfast might settle at
the gentle gait we are going, but
shortly he says, " It 's sixty miles,
and we must move along." We
break into a gallop. The landscape
is gilded by the morning sun, and
the cool of the October air makes it
a perfect thing, but there are ele-
ments in the affair which complicate
its perfection. The " bad lands "
are rough, and the general goes
down a hill with even more rapidity
than up it. The horses are not the
perfect animals of the bridle-path,

but poor old cavalry brutes, procured by the government under the old contract system, by which the government pays something like $125 for a $60 horse. This could be remedied by allowing the officers of each regiment to buy their own horses; but in our army nothing is remedied, because a lot of nice old gentlemen in Washington are too conservative to do anything but eat and sleep. There is a bit of human nature at the bottom of our army organization, and where is the man who can change that? Men who were the very jewels of the profession years ago have reached in due time the upper grades of rank, and occupy the bureaus of the department. These men who have acquired rank, years, and discretion naturally do nothing, and with sedate gravity insist that no one else shall do anything. The ambitious young men have to wait patiently for their retirement, and in process of waiting they, too, become old and conservative. Old soldiers are pardonable rubbish, since soldiers, like other men, must age and decay, the only distinction being that youthful vigor is of prime importance to a soldier, while in the case of the citizen any abatement of vigor is rewarded by being shelved. What to do with old soldiers is a problem which I will hand over to the economists as being beyond my depth. But to return to the going downhill. General Miles has acquired his knowledge of riding from wild Indians, and wild Indians go uphill and downhill as a matter of course at whatever gait they happen to be travelling. He would make his horse climb a tree with equal gravity if he was bound that way. The general has known Indians to ride for two days and a night at a rapid gallop, and it never occurs to him that he cannot do

anything which any one else can; so
he spurs along, and we go cutting
around the *coulies* and bluffs like
frightened antelopes or mad creatures. The escort strings out behind.
This is observed with a grim humor
by the general, who desires nothing
so much as to leave his escort far in
the rear. He turns in his saddle,
and seeing the dust of the escort far
behind, says: "Shake up the young
men a little; do 'em good. They
get sleepy"; and away we go.

It is over thirty miles to the first
relay station, or courier's camp, and
another problem looms up. The
general's weight is over two hundred
pounds, and I confess to two hundred and fifteen avoirdupois, and, as
I have before remarked, my horse
was not an Irish hunter, so my mus-
ing took a serious vein. It is all
very well for a major-general to ride
down a cavalry horse, but if such an
accident were to happen to me, then

my friends in the cavalry would
crown me with thorns. Two hundred
and fifteen pounds requires a great
deal more careful attention than a
one-hundred-and-forty-pound wasp-
waisted cavalryman. What the latter can do with impunity would put
me on foot—a thing that happened
some ten years since in this very
State of Montana, and a thing I
have treasured in mind, and will not
have repeated. So I brought the
old horse down to a trot, and a good
round trot eats up a road in short
order. Your galloper draws away
from you, but if the road is long
enough, you find that you are at his
heels.

After a good day's ride of something like sixty miles, we met a troop
of the Eighth Cavalry near its camp
on the Tongue River, and the general is escorted in. The escorts
draw into line, salute, and the general is duly deposited in a big Sibley

tent; and I go away on the arms of some "cavalry kids" (as young lieutenants are called) to a hole in the ground (a dugout) where they are quartered. On the following morning I am duly admonished that if my whereabouts could have been ascertained on the previous evening, the expedition would have continued to the camp of the First Cavalry. I do not think the general was unduly severe, desiring simply to shift the responsibility of the procrastination on to other shoulders, and meanwhile being content to have things as they were. I was privately thanked by the citizen members of the commission for the delay I had caused, since they had a well-grounded conviction that sixty miles a day in an army ambulance was trouble enough. After some sarcasm by a jolly young sub, to the effect that " if one wants to call a citizen out of a tent, one must ring a dinner - bell,'' we were again mounted and on the way. I was badly mounted that day, but able to participate in the wild charge of forty-five miles to the Lame Deer camp, near the Cheyenne Agency. The fifty Cheyenne scouts and a troop of the Eighth were in escort.

By a happy combination I was able to add greatly to my equestrian knowledge on this ride. It happened in this way; but I must explain. Some years ago I had occasion to ride a stock saddle (the cowboy article), and with all the positiveness of immature years, I held all other trees and all other methods of riding in a magnificent contempt. Later on I had to be convinced that a great many young cavalry officers in our service were the most daring and perfect riders, and that the McClelland saddle was the proper thing. I even elaborated a theory in explanation of all this, which I had duly shattered for me when I came East and frequented a New York riding-academy, where a smiling professor of the art assured me that cowboys and soldiers were the worst possible riders. Indeed, the sneers of the polite European were so superlative that I dared not even doubt his statements. Of course I never quite understood how my old champions of the cattle range and the war trail could pick things off the ground while in full career, or ride like mad over the cut banks and bowlders, if they were such desperately bad riders; and I never was able to completely understand why my European master could hardly turn in his saddle without tumbling off. But still he reduced me to submission, and I ceased even to doubt. I changed my style of riding, in deference to a public sentiment, and got my legs tucked up under my chin, and learned to loose my seat at

83

every alternate footfall, and in time acquired a balance which was as secure as a pumpkin on the side of a barrel. Thus equipped with all this knowledge and my own saddle, I went out to the Northwest with the purpose of introducing a little revolution in cavalry riding. Things went swimmingly for a time. The interpreters and scouts watched my riding with mingled pity and scorn, but I knew they were unenlightened, and in no way to be regarded seriously. The general was duly amused by my teetering, and suggested to the smiling escort officers that " he has lived so long abroad, you know," etc., all of which I did not mind, for my faith in the eternal art of the thing was complete. Now to tell how I discovered that I was riding a seat which was no seat at all, and was only retained by a series of happy accidents, I will continue. While at the head of the column, where I could see the deep ruts in the road and the bowlders, and could dodge the prairie-dog holes, it was simple enough; but my horse being a very clumsy galloper, and beginning to blow under the pace, I began to pull up, calculating to get a sharp trot, and overhaul the column when it slowed down. The column of soldiers dashed by, and the great cloud of dust rose up behind them which always follows a herd of animals in the West. Being no longer able to see, the only thing to do under the circumstances was to give my horse his head, and resign myself to the chances of a gopher hole, if it was foreordained that my horse should find one. True to his instincts, my old cavalry horse plunged into the ranks. You cannot keep a troop horse out of the ranks. They know their place, and seek it with the exactitude of water. If the cavalry tactics are ever

85

changed, the present race of horses will have to be sold, because, while you can teach a horse anything, you cannot unteach him.

In front I could see two silhouettes of soldiers tearing along, and behind could hear the heavy pounding of the troop horses, the clank of arms, the snorts and heavy breathings. I could hardly see my horse's head, to say nothing of the ground in front. Here is where the perfect grip with the thighs is wanted, and here is where the man who is bundled up like a ball on his horse's back is in imminent danger of breaking his neck. I felt like a pack on a government mule, and only wished I had some one to " throw the diamond hitch over me." The inequalities of the road make your horse plunge and go staggering sidewise, or down on his knees, and it is not at all an unusual thing for a cavalryman to upset entirely, though nothing short

86

of a total turn-over will separate a veteran soldier from his horse. After a few miles of these vicissitudes I gained the head of the column, and when the pace slackened I turned the whole thing over in my mind, and a great light seemed to shine through the whole subject. For a smooth road and a trotting horse, that European riding-master was right; but when you put a man in the dust or smoke, over the rocks and cut banks, on the " bucking " horse, or where he must handle his weapons or his *vieta*, he must have a seat on his mount as tight as a stamp on an envelope, and not go washing around like a shot in a bottle. In a park or on a country road, where a man has nothing to do but give his undivided attention to sticking on his saddle, it has its advantages. An Indian or a cowboy could take the average park rider off from his horse, scalp him, hang him on a bush, and never break a gallop. I do not wish to seem intolerant, because I will say that the most beautiful horse and the most perfect horseman I have ever seen was the bay gelding Partisan and his rider in the high-school class at the recent Horse Show in New York; but I do insist that no one shall for a moment imagine that the American style of riding is not the firmest of all seats.

With a repetition of the military forms, we reached the cavalry camp on the Lame Deer Creek. This is an old battle-ground of the general's —his last fight with the Cheyennes, where, as the general puts it, we "kicked them out of their blankets in the early morning." These Indians recognize him as their conqueror, and were allied with him in the Nez Percé campaign. One old chief pointed to the stars on his shoulder-strap, and charged him to remember that they helped to put them there.

That night was very cold, and I slept badly, so at an early hour I rolled out of my blankets and crawled into my clothes. I stepped out of my tent, and saw that the stars were yet visible and the light of the morning warming up to chase the gray shadows over the western hills. Three tight little cavalry soldiers came out on the parade, and blew three bugles as hard as ever they could to an unappreciative audience of sleepy soldiers and solemn hills. I walked down past the officers' row, and shook the kinks out of my stiffened knees. Everything was as quietly dismal as only a sleeping camp can be. The Sibley containing General Miles showed no signs of life, and until he arose this little military solar system would not revolve. I bethought me of the irregulars. They were down in the river bottom—Lieutenant Casey and his Indian scouts. I knew that Casey had commanded Indian scouts until his temper was as refined as beaten gold, so I thought it safer to arouse him than any one else, and, walking down, I scratched at his tent—which is equivalent to knocking—and received a rather loud and surly inquiry as to what I wanted. My sensitive nature was so shocked by this that, like the bad actor, I had hopes for no more generous gift than a cigarette. I was let into the Sibley, and saw the ground covered with blanketed forms. One of the swathed forms sat up, and the captain allowed he wanted to get up in the night, but that ever since Lieutenant Blank had shot at the orderly he was afraid to move about in the gloom. Lieutenant B. sat up and denied the impeachment. Another officer arose and made some extended remarks on the unseemly disturbance at this unseasonable hour. To pass over these inequalities of life, I will say that the military process of stiffening a man's backbone and reducing his mind to a logarithm breeds a homogeneous class whom we all know. They have small waists, and their clothes fit them; they are punctilious; they respect forms, and always do the dignified and proper thing at the particular instant, and never display their individuality except on two occasions: one is the field of battle and the other is before breakfast. Some bright fellow will one day tell in print the droll stock anecdotes of the United States army, and you 'll all agree that they are good. They are better, though, if you sit in a Sibley on a cold morning while the orderly boils the coffee; and are more fortunate if you have Ned Casey to embellish what he calls the international complications which arose from the bombardment of

Canada with paving-stones by a drunken recruit at Detroit.

After the commission had talked to a ring of drowsy old chiefs, and the general had reminded them that he had thrashed them once, and was perfectly willing to do it again if they did not keep in the middle of the big road, the commission was loaded into the ambulance. The driver clucked and whistled and snapped his whip as a preliminary which always precedes the concerted movement of six mules, and we started. This time I found that I had a mount that was " a horse from the ground up," as they phrase it in the red-blooded West. Well it was so, for at the relay camp I had issued to me a sorrel ruin which in the pristine vigor of its fifth year would not have commanded the value of a tin cup. After doing a mile of song and dance on this poor beast I dismounted, and shifting my saddle back to my led horse of the morning, which was led by a Crow scout, made the sixty-mile march of that day on the noble animal. Poor old chap, fit for a king, good for all day and the next, would bring six hundred dollars in the New York Horse Exchange, but condemned to pack a trooper in the ranks until a penurious government condemns and sells him to a man who, nine times out of ten, by the law of God, ought not to be intrusted with the keeping of the meanest of his creatures, to say nothing of his noblest work—a horse. " Such is life," is the salve a good soldier puts on his wounds.

During the day we went all over the battle-field of the Little Big Horn. I heard a good deal of professional criticism, and it is my settled conviction that had Reno and Benteen gone in and fought as hard as they were commanded to do, Custer would have won his fight, and to-day be a major-general. The military moral of that affair for young soldiers is that when in doubt about what to do it is always safe to go in and fight " till you drop," remembering that, however a citizen may regard the proposition, a soldier cannot afford to be anything else than a " dead lion."

We were nearing the Crow Agency and Fort Custer, and it is against all my better impulses, and with trepidation at the impropriety of unveiling the truth, that I disclose the fact that the general would halt the column at a convenient distance from a post, and would then exchange his travel-worn garb for glittering niceties of a major-general's uniform. The command then advanced into the fort. The guns bellowed and the cavalry swung into line, while numerous officers gathered, in all the perfection of neatfitting uniforms, to receive him. At

this time the writer eliminated himself from the ceremonial, and from
some point of vantage proceeded to
pull up his boots so as to cover as
much as possible the gaping wounds
in his riding-trousers, and tried
vainly to make a shooting-jacket fit
like an officer's blouse, while he
dealt his hat sundry thumps in a
vain endeavor to give it a more rak-
ish appearance. He was then in-
troduced and apologized for in turn.
To this day he hopes the mantle of
charity was broad enough to cover
his case.

What a contrast between soldiers
in field and soldiers in garrison!
Natty and trim—as straight as a
sapling, with few words and no ges-
tures—quite unlike those of two
days, or rather nights, ago, when
the cold froze them out of their
blankets, and they sat around the
camp-fires pounding tin cans and
singing the Indian medicine song

with a good Irish accent. Very
funny that affair—the mixture of
Cheyenne and Donnybrook is a
strange noise.

The last stage from Custer to the
railroad is thirty-five miles and a
half, which we did with two relays,
the latter half of it in the night.
There was no escort—only two order-
lies and the general—and I pattered
along through the gloom. The
clouds hung over the earth in a
dense blanket, and the road was as
dim as a Florentine fresco; but night
nor cold nor heat can bring General
Miles to a walk, and the wild charge
in the dark was, as an experience, a
complete thing. You cannot see;
you whirl through a cañon cut in
the mud; you plough through the
sage-brush and over the rocks clatter
and bang. The general is certainly
a grim old fellow—one of the kind
that makes sparks fly when he strikes
an obstacle. I could well believe

the old Fifth Infantryman who said " he 's put many a corn on a dough-boy's foot," and it 's a red-letter day for any one else that keeps at his horse's heels. You may ride into a hole, over a precipice, to per-dition, if it 's your luck on this night, but is not the general in front ? You follow the general—that 's the grand idea—that is the military idea. If the United States army was strung out in line with its general ahead, and if he should ride out into the broad Atlantic and swim to sea, the whole United States army would follow along, for that 's the idea, you know.

But for the headlong plunge of an orderly, we passed through all right, with due thankfulness on my part, and got to our car at the sid-ing, much to the gratification of the Chicago colored man in charge, who found life at Custer Station a horrid blank. Two hundred and

G

97

forty-eight miles in thirty-six hours and a half, and sixty miles of it on one horse, was not bad riding, considering everything. Not enough to make a man famous or lame, but enough for the time being.

THE END